ST. JOHN'S LUTHERAN
ELEMENTARY SCHOOL
For a Christ-Centered Education
3521 Linda Vista Ave.
Napa, California

The Mystery of
Pony Hollow Panda

The Mystery of
Pony Hollow Panda

By Lynn Hall

Illustrated by William Hutchinson

GARRARD PUBLISHING COMPANY
CHAMPAIGN, ILLINOIS

Library of Congress Cataloging in Publication Data

Hall, Lynn.
    The Mystery of Pony Hollow Panda.

    (A Garrard mystery book)
    Summary: When her pony disappears from the pet parade,
Sarah follows the clues and tries to unravel the mystery.
    [1. Mystery and detective stories. 2. Ponies—Fic-
tion] I. Hutchinson, William M., ill. II. Title.
    PZ7.H1458Myb   [Fic]   81-6389
    ISBN 0-8116-6416-3   AACR2

Contents

1. A Shadow across the Sun

The morning sun slanted over the trees and warmed Sarah's back. Its heat felt good, for her arms and legs were cold and wet from the hose she held.

It was Memorial Day—too early in the summer for cold water to feel good at eight o'clock in the morning. But it was Pet Fair day, marking the end of the school year, and Panda couldn't be in a parade and pet show without a bath.

Sarah and Panda stood outside the rambling old pony stable. Panda was tied to the fence, her head hanging almost to her knees. Her lower lip hung loose, as though she were resigned to the bath, but not to liking it.

Sarah was barefoot, her shirt sleeves and jeans legs rolled up as high as they could go. Her shirt was soaked, and soapsuds ran in little white trains down her face and legs. Panda had just shaken herself and splattered shampoo in every direction.

The kitchen door of the farmhouse opened, and Sarah's mother came across the yard. A small plastic bottle was in her hand. She was not much taller than Sarah, and she had the same brownish-blond hair as her daughter. All of her movements seemed full of energy and purpose, as though she always knew what she was doing and why. She made Sarah feel aimless and witless sometimes, by comparison.

Mrs. Elgin held out the plastic bottle. "Try some of this in the rinse water, Sary."

"What is it? Bluing! I don't want her to turn blue, mom."

"She won't. Just put about three squirts in a bucket of rinse water and pour it over her. It'll make her white parts nice and bright."

Sarah took the bottle doubtfully. "You're sure it won't turn her blue?"

"Not just three squirts. You're going to be gorgeous, Pandy," Mrs. Elgin said as she patted the pony. "Chin up, the worst is over."

Mrs. Elgin sat on the fence, some distance away, in case the pony shook herself again.

"I wonder if they ever gave baths to the mine ponies," she said. "They must have gotten pretty dirty, working in coal mines all day."

Sarah put three squirts of bluing into her bucket and began filling it with water from the hose. She looked around her, at the pony stable where the mine ponies had lived years ago and at the steep face of the hill that rose just beyond the farm buildings. An old wooden door led into the hillside, into the abandoned Makenna coal mine whose tunnels wandered mysteriously beneath the farm.

Sarah's family had just bought the farm last winter, but already Sarah loved it more than any place she had ever known. Although the mine entrance was sealed shut, for safety, Sarah liked knowing there were miles of unexplored tunnels under her feet.

She loved the pony stable for the ghosts of past ponies who had lived there, for the home it gave her own well-loved Panda, and for the dreams it held, of future ponies to be bred and owned by Sarah Elgin, pony breeder.

In a rambling, forested ravine beyond the hay field was a place called Pony Hollow. It was special to Sarah in a way that no one else fully understood. There, in a tiny stone cottage almost hidden by vines, Sarah had found the skeleton of Oberon. He was a Connemara stallion who had been hidden there and left to die, by a man who was trapped in circumstances he couldn't fight. Many years later, it had been Sarah who had eased the man's lifelong guilt and released Oberon's spirit.

"Watch it," Mrs. Elgin said sharply.

The bucket was overflowing, spilling blue water on Sarah's feet.

"Here goes," Sarah said, as she picked up the bucket and began to pour the water over Panda's back. She stood back and looked. The pony wasn't turning blue. Moving with more assurance now, Sarah sloshed the rest of the water over Panda's white-booted legs and down the white blaze on the pony's face.

"Hey, mom, you were right. That bluing really does brighten up her white parts."

Sarah moved in closer to Panda with the hose and began the final rinse. Then she ran her hand down the pony's glossy black hip, to get off as much water as possible. Suddenly she stopped and frowned.

"What's this?" she said, half aloud and half to herself. Sarah lay the hose on the ground so she would have both hands to examine Panda's hip.

Her fingers found and traced a long welt that ran from the point of Panda's hip, down and back across the pony's rump.

"What is the matter?" Mrs. Elgin jumped down from the fence and came for a closer look.

The wet black hairs of Panda's coat separated to reveal the welt, thin, pale, and hairless. It had been hidden till then by the pony's thick coat.

"It's a scar," Mrs. Elgin said.

"A scar? You mean somebody whipped her? Somebody whipped my Pandy?"

"Whatever happened to her, she wasn't yours then," Sarah's mother said.

"I know it, but that doesn't make any difference. Panda's so good. She always does what I want her to. Why would anybody ever whip her? They should be whipped themselves." Her voice cracked with anger.

"Now, cool down, there. You don't know that she was whipped. She might have been cut by wire or have been in some other accident. Panda is yours now, so you know she's not going to be mistreated in the future."

"I'm going to find out what happened to Panda," Sarah announced. "If someone is going around whipping ponies, I'm going to make him stop."

Her mother gave a light tug to Sarah's ponytail, as if to say, "You aren't really serious." Then she started back toward the house. "Better work fast," she called to Sarah. "You don't want to be late for the parade."

Sarah scowled after her. "You don't think I mean it," she muttered, "but I do."

She went back to work on Panda. She dried the pony's face and wiped off her hooves. The morning was going fast, Sarah suddenly realized. She still had to braid the feathers into Panda's mane and tail. She had to get herself bathed and into her costume.

It would take some time to ride the mile and a half into town. Since the parade started at noon, and the pet fair at one o'clock, she had no time to waste.

Sarah paused for one more thoughtful moment, her fingers tracing the scar. It was disappearing from sight now, for the sun was drying Panda's back. The wet hairs were no longer plastered to the pony's skin.

A dark mood came over Sarah, as though a cloud had blown across the sun. She felt, without knowing why, that something bad was coming.

2. Pet Fair and Panic

Sandy River was typical of the small towns in southern Iowa. Its center was a block-square park surrounded by the main businesses of the town. Scattered among the huge old oak trees were a bandstand, a tall bronze plaque listing the men who had died in World War I, three drinking fountains, and a flagpole surrounded by marigolds and Indian paintbrush plants.

The Memorial Day Pet Parade had started.

It was moving slowly, from the elementary school two blocks away, to the park. This parade was for children only.

It was led by Marcy Hamilton, a high school student in Arabian costume, who was riding one of her parents' Arabian horses. She was not really an adult but was old enough to be responsible for leading the parade.

Behind Marcy came a half dozen recruits from the elementary school percussion band.

They were banging and clanging on triangles, cymbals, and small drums.

Then came the bigger pets. Panda carried Sarah the Indian princess and two smaller ponies carried very small cowboys, while a tiny shaggy donkey pulled a cart with three young children in it. Two of them were grinning and waving, the third was crying and wanting to get off.

Then came the dogs. Zeke Van Horn led a

huge Irish wolfhound dressed as a horse. The dog had a tiny but genuine pony saddle on his back. A small girl in a nurse's costume pushed a doll buggy decorated as a Red Cross ambulance. Over the edge of the buggy peered a sad, bandaged bulldog. A boxer had a kerchief around his neck and a pirate patch over one eye. The other dogs were not dressed up.

Small children marched while trying to hold cats in their arms. Others carried cages of fluttering birds or cowering hamsters. A few marched with fish bowls. They walked with their heads down, watching the water, so they wouldn't spill it.

The parade was a lively sight as it made its way around the town square. There was much noise—clanging, banging, weeping, barking, yowling, and calls to mommies and to friends. The sidewalks were lined with grinning watchers who nudged each other and said, "Look, isn't that one cute?"

Sarah enjoyed herself completely. She forgot

scars and whips and dark forebodings. In the back of her mind she knew that she would soon be too old to dress up, to pretend, but that only made today more precious.

She wore a short, fringed dress of tan material that looked a little like leather. Her mother had made the fringes and decorated the front with beads. Feathers from Sarah's colorful bantam rooster decorated Sarah's long braid of hair and Panda's mane and tail. Now and then, when she thought of it, Sarah put her fingers to her mouth and made some sounds that she imagined sounded like an Indian calling. "Wu-wu-wu-wu." As she rode she looked around and grinned.

After circling the park, the parade stopped at the bandstand. When the parade disbanded, Sarah slid down from Panda's back and tied her reins to a park bench.

"There now, you can rest here in the shade till it's time for the show," Sarah said, running her hand down Panda's mane.

Sarah looked up suddenly, for she felt that someone was watching her. She spotted a pleasant-looking young woman who stood a few yards away. The woman smiled at both Sarah and Panda, but her smile lingered on the pony.

"Hello, Panda," the woman said softly.

Sarah started to ask the woman how she knew Panda's name, but just then Zeke Van Horn raced by, yelling, "Grab him, somebody!"

The Irish wolfhound was racing through the park, his saddle sideways and his stirrups bounding in the air. Just ahead of him streaked a cat in doll clothes. The cat's owner, a little girl with red scratches on her arm, was close behind the wolfhound. She was trying to grab the dog and was yelling at him to leave her cat alone.

Sarah and Zeke closed in on the wolfhound and dragged him to a halt just as the cat started to climb a tree. Zeke tripped and Sarah

fell over him, so the children and dog landed in a tangle of legs and feet and paws.

"You okay?" Zeke puffed as he struggled to get up from the bottom of the pile.

"Yeah. Your dog's got his foot in my face—there, ouch, okay, there. Here are your glasses." Sarah handed Zeke his glasses, and then he pulled Sarah to her feet.

The cat's owner stood at the base of the tree and looked up at her pet, whose eyes were flashing. The doll bonnet was hanging sideways over the cat's face. It was all Sarah could do to keep from laughing.

"Want me to get your cat down?" Zeke offered.

"No, just get that monster away from here. Petronius isn't going to come down as long as he can see that dog."

Zeke turned to Sarah and shrugged. He was a sturdy, squarely-built boy with a spot of white hair the size of a silver dollar on the side of his head. Sarah had noticed him at school, although he wasn't in her room, but until today she hadn't talked to him.

"Thanks for helping," he said. "I knew we were in for it, as soon as Max saw that cat. I'm pretty strong for my age, but then, so is he." He laughed and showed Sarah his hands, where the dog's rope had burned off the skin. Sarah decided she liked Zeke Van Horn.

Zeke said, "You rode that black pony with the white legs, didn't you? That's really a pretty pony."

Sarah was sure she liked him.

"Her name is Panda," she said. "You can ride her sometime if you want to."

"Yeah!" Zeke's eyes widened with pleasure. "You don't live too far from us—about a mile. We live in the big green house, just north of town. There's a sign in the yard, 'Lawnmower Repairs.' "

"I know where that is," Sarah said. "We live at the old Makenna—oh, you knew that already."

"I always liked that place. Maybe I'll come over sometime and ride your pony."

"Okay." Sarah thought that would be nice.

They stopped near the bandstand to listen as the announcer explained how the pet show would be run. He was from the local merchants' club, which sponsored the pet show. Other club members moved through the crowd and pinned numbers on children. They explained about the classes.

Sarah got her number. She was entered in the Horses and Ponies Class and in the contest for Best Costume.

Classes for the younger children were held first. Sarah and Zeke watched the children six and under. Then Sarah said, "I'd better go make sure Panda is okay. See you later."

She ran around the bandstand and moved through the crowd toward Panda's bench.

Panda was gone.

3. Vanished!

"She couldn't have disappeared," said Sarah's mother for the third time. "Don't worry, honey, we'll find her."

The park had become a nightmare for Sarah. All she could think about was her beloved Panda. Where could she be? Sarah moved her head this way and that as she strained for the sight of Panda.

Her father went to the announcer and spoke to him. A minute later, from the loudspeakers above the bandstand, came the announcement. "We've got a lost pony, folks. It's a black pony with white legs and Indian feathers. Anyone seeing this pony, please bring her to the bandstand. Thank you."

Sarah began to tremble. Everyone was treating this as though Panda had become untied and had wandered off, as though she'd reappear any minute now.

But Sarah knew better. Without knowing why she was so certain, Sarah *knew* Panda hadn't wandered off by herself. She'd been stolen. She might even be in danger. There was every chance that she might be gone for good. "Why would anyone want to take Panda?" Sarah asked herself numbly.

The feeling Sarah remembered from the morning, the feeling of a cloud passing across the sun, was back now, stronger and darker than before. Sarah realized that this must be the trouble she had sensed was coming. Sarah wasn't sure she could stand it.

She felt her mother's hand on her shoulder. It was just the support she needed.

"You run and look for her, honey. I'll stay here by the bandstand in case someone finds her and brings her back."

Sarah ran, grateful for something to do. Suddenly Zeke was there. "Is it your pony that's lost? I heard the announcement."

"Yeah."

Without a word Zeke joined Sarah in the search. They circled the park together, stopping now and then to stand on a bench so they could see over the heads of all the people.

"Has a black and white pony come by here?" they asked over and over. People shook their heads or said a kindly, "No."

It was soon clear that Panda was not in the park.

After checking with her mother to be sure that no one had returned Panda, Sarah set off again with Zeke to search the streets near the park. They looked into garages and alleys. They asked old people sitting on porches if they had seen a pony go by. There were no clues. No one had seen Panda.

Two hours later Sarah and Zeke finally gave up and returned to the bandstand. By now the pet show was over and the park nearly empty. Sarah's mother was sitting on the steps of the empty bandstand and looking anxiously around her. She smiled when she saw Sarah.

"No luck?" she asked as Sarah walked wearily across the trampled grass.

Sarah shook her head. She didn't trust her voice. Her tears were too near the surface.

"Where's dad?" she managed to say.

"He went over to the police station to notify the police. They'll find her. Someone is bound to call them any time now and report a pony in their flower garden or something."

"Maybe somebody already has," Sarah said, but she didn't believe it. Panda was stolen. The knowledge was like a weight inside her.

She raised her hands and waved them helplessly. "I don't see how Panda could have gotten out of this crowded park without somebody seeing her. It's impossible. If she was loose and wandering around, surely somebody would have called for help, or reported that a pony was loose. But *nobody* saw *anything.*"

"I know," her mother said. "I don't understand that either. Here comes dad. Maybe he's found out something."

He did not have any news. Sarah could tell that by the way he walked. When he came up to them, he shook his head and said, "They haven't had any calls yet, but they'll let us know as soon as they hear something."

He looked at Sarah and his wife. "Well, let's get on home," he said abruptly. "There's nothing more we can do here. The police will call us at home when they find her."

That evening and all the next day, Sarah stayed near the phone, willing it to ring.

The police did not call.

Several times during the day, the announcer at the local radio station broadcast this announcement: "A lost pony, strayed from the Sandy River city park yesterday afternoon. It is black with a white face and feet, about thirteen hands tall, and answers to the name 'Panda.' Anyone who has seen this pony please call 767-3645. Folks, we've got a pretty worried little girl looking for her pony."

By the second day Sarah could no longer stand to be near the telephone, which did not ring to bring her good news. Instead she spent the day on her bike, riding up and down streets in town and dirt roads at the edge of town. She searched everywhere she went and asked anyone she could find if they had seen her pony.

That night, tired by her search and her grief, Sarah sank into a deep sleep, and dreamed unhappy dreams.

4. Night Message

When Sarah woke, the mood of her dreams was still with her. She didn't remember all of the dream scenes, but one impression stayed. Panda was back in her former home, wherever that was.

Sarah rolled about, tangling the blankets around her legs. "Why would I think that?" she wondered. "I don't even know where Panda lived before. She was happy here, I know she was. But still—" her mind raced. "Still, what if she did wander away from the park? She wouldn't know how to find her way back here. She hadn't lived here long enough. But she might know her way back to her old home, if it was somewhere close to town. Maybe she is back there now!"

Sarah kicked off the covers and ran to her parents' room across the hall. They were still asleep.

"Daddy, were you about to wake up?" Sarah asked, as she jiggled the bed.

"Mmfg." He turned his face into the pillow.

"It's important, daddy. Do you think you could wake up for just a minute?"

From the other side of the bed, Mrs. Elgin said, "What's the matter, honey?"

"I need to know something. I have an idea. Daddy, you told me you bought Panda at an auction sale. Would the people there know where she lived before?"

Mrs. Elgin was sitting up now, and Mr.

Elgin had his face out of the pillow and one eye open.

He yawned and said, "I'm sure they'd have it in their records, Sary. Why? What are you thinking?"

"Well," she settled herself on the bed. "I thought if Panda did get loose from the park and wander away, that she might have gone back to her old home. If she lived there for a long time, she'd remember it a lot better than she would here, because we had her for only a few months. Where was the sale place?"

"It was, um," he rubbed his face, and his morning whiskers sounded scratchy against his hand. "It was the A & J Livestock Auction, out on the highway east of town, across from the Dairy Dreem. It wouldn't hurt to check with them, if you want to."

Sarah bounced out of the room. Mrs. Elgin looked sadly at her husband. "It's not going to do any good."

He yawned. "Probably not, hon, but at least

it'll give the poor kid something to do. She has been so lost without Panda."

All morning Sarah called the phone number of the livestock auction. No one answered. Finally, unable to stay in the house any longer, she wheeled her bike out of the garage and rode the three miles to the auction barn. It was just across the highway from the Dairy Dreem Drive-in, where her family sometimes stopped for cones.

The office part of the huge white building was locked and empty, but Sarah found a man working among the pens in the back. He was a wiry little man in western boots and hat. He was carrying hay to some calves in one of the pens.

"Mornin', sis," he said. "What can I do for you?"

"I'm trying to find out something. My daddy bought a pony here two months ago. Could you look up in the records and see who she used to belong to?"

"I reckon I could. Hold on a minute while I finish up with these calves, and I'll see if I can find that for you."

She waited, but she became more impatient by the second. At last he led the way into the main barn and fished the office key out of his pocket.

"Now, when did you say that would have been, sis?"

"The end of March."

"Okay. We have a horse auction the last Friday of every month, so that would have been—right here." He opened a huge ledger book. "What's your father's name?"

"Norm Elgin." Sarah held her breath while the man went through the ledger.

"Sure thing. Here it is. Black pony mare, named Panda. The seller, J.G. Pringle, Albia. The buyer, Norman Elgin, Sandy River. That's what you wanted to know, sis?"

Sarah nodded, but her spirits sank. Albia was forty miles away. Panda couldn't have found her way back there. She fought back tears of disappointment. Then the man wrote Pringle's name and address on a scrap of paper, and Sarah accepted it and thanked him for his trouble.

The bike ride home seemed endless. Sarah had forgotten to eat lunch before she started for the sale barn. She arrived home hungry, weary, dusty, and deeply discouraged.

When she told her mother that Panda had come from Albia, not from Sandy River, Mrs. Elgin said, "Why not give the people a call, honey? It can't hurt."

Sarah just shook her head. She was too tired to face any more disappointment.

"Well," her mother said briskly, "I've got a dentist's appointment in half an hour. Want to come along? I'll take you for a Dairy Dreem cone afterward."

Sarah shook her head.

She wandered around the house after her mother left. She tried to read her library book, but she couldn't get her mind away from Panda.

Finally she went to the phone and dialed information.

A few minutes later she was speaking to Mrs. Pringle, in Albia. She told the woman why she was calling.

"Oh, that wasn't our pony, dear," the voice said kindly. "My husband just took the pony to the auction as a favor. He has a truck. The pony belonged to my sister, there in Sandy River. You must have heard about their fire, I'm sure."

"What fire?" Sarah asked. Hope surged in her again. Panda *was* from Sandy River after all.

"Why, the Bowen fire, of course. You must have heard about it, last fall. My sister's husband and daughter died in the fire. My sister was hospitalized from the shock of it. Naturally she didn't want to have to look at that pony and be reminded. So my husband went and got the pony, and we kept it here a while and then took it down to the March horse auction."

Sarah thanked the woman and hung up, dazed by this new knowledge. The Bowen fire—of course.

It had happened just after Sarah's family moved to Sandy River. Julie Bowen had been in the grade below Sarah's, so Sarah hadn't known her. In fact, at the time, Sarah was still trying to learn the names of everyone in her own class.

But she did remember, clearly, the principal's voice coming over the intercom to every room in the school. He had announced, in a quiet voice that trembled just a bit, that Julie Bowen had died the evening before, in a fire at her home. Her funeral would be Wednesday. Anyone wishing to attend would be excused from school. Then he asked for a moment of silent prayer. Through that endless, silent moment, Sarah stared at her desk top,

terribly afraid of something she didn't under-stand.

And now that unknown, dead girl was a part of Sarah's life. She had been Panda's owner. Maybe, Sarah thought, that connection might somehow point the way to Panda.

"Mom and the car are gone," Sarah said to herself. "I don't know where Mrs. Bowen lived. Zeke. He'll know. He'll help."

She was already out of the house, on her bike, pedaling furiously toward Zeke's house.

5. A Smiling Face

Zeke was eager to go with Sarah when she told him what she'd learned. His mother remembered the fire. She didn't know exactly where the Bowen family had lived, but she knew the street, and the block. One of the women in her bridge club lived in the same block.

As they left the house, Zeke said, "If Panda had come back, wouldn't Mrs. Bowen have reported it to the police or someone?"

"I don't know," Sarah said. "Probably. But her sister, the woman I talked to in Albia, said something about Mrs. Bowen being in the hospital after the fire. Maybe she's still in the hospital, or sick in bed, or something. Maybe Panda is wandering around near her house, and Mrs. Bowen doesn't even know it. Maybe I'm just crazy, and the whole thing is a dumb idea."

"Oh well," Zeke said, grinning. "I guess it beats sitting home not doing anything to try to find Panda."

"That's the way I feel. Here. This is the street, isn't it? Mulberry Street?"

It was an area of small houses set in very large yards, on a quiet blacktopped road at the edge of town. There were no sidewalks here, and rural mailboxes lined the streets. It was a neighborhood for children and horses and dogs, boats on trailers beside garages, old cars on blocks in side yards. Behind the large yards was open country.

As Zeke and Sarah pedaled slowly down the block to the end, they found where the Bowen house had been. A blackened chimney still stood, a grim reminder of the tragedy. At the end of the street, the road widened in a turn-around. Beyond the road was a bean field.

The Bowen property was similar to all the others on the block. A high lilac hedge bordered the yard and half-hid it from the neighbors. Large trees dotted the lawn, and around the edges were peony bushes heavy with pink and white blooms.

In the center of the yard, where the house should have been, there was only the chimney and a blackened rim of a house foundation. Behind the house foundation, Sarah could see the roof of a small building, a shed or garage of some sort.

Near the spot where the house had been stood a small silver house trailer. Sarah could hear the sound of a television coming from inside it.

"Should we go up and knock?" Zeke asked.

"I guess so, now that we're here. But what should we say?" Faced with the need to do something, Sarah felt suddenly foolish. She didn't know why they'd come. Still, Zeke was watching her, waiting for her to decide. It was her pony, after all. It was her search. She had to do something.

She said, "I'll just go up and ask if they've seen Panda. I'll say I lost my pony and I'm making a house to house search to see if anybody remembers seeing her. That wouldn't sound too dumb, I guess."

"I'll stay here and keep watch," Zeke whispered to her. Playing detective had become a game between them. Somehow that made it easier for Sarah to go up to the door of the trailer and knock.

A young woman opened the door. Her face was familiar. For an instant Sarah felt taken aback, confused. Oh, yes. This was the same woman she'd seen in the park the day of the

pet show, the one who had called Panda by name.

"Hello," the woman said pleasantly. "What can I do for you this morning? Are you selling Girl Scout cookies?"

Sarah's mind went blank. She forgot what she was going to say. Her mind was full of the picture of this woman standing beside Panda, right before Panda had disappeared.

"Yes, what is it?" The woman spoke again, still kindly, as though she understood tongue-tied children.

Sarah found her words. "I'm sorry to bother you, but I'm looking for my pony. She disappeared from the park on Memorial Day, and I haven't found her yet. I'm asking everybody in town if they remember seeing her, or have seen her since."

"A pony? No, I'm sorry, I'm afraid I can't help you."

The woman began to fade back into the inside of the trailer.

"She used to be yours. Panda. I thought she might have found her way back here," Sarah said quickly.

"I haven't seen her," the woman said, and her face seemed to soften. "I hope you find her. My daughter has a pony like that, so I can imagine how fond you are of yours. Well, good luck. I hope you find your pony."

The door closed, and Sarah could do nothing but turn and go back to where Zeke waited.

"What did she say?" he demanded.

Sarah just shook her head. "I don't understand it. She talked as though her daughter was still alive. She said, 'My daughter *has* a pony like that,' *not* 'had a pony.' It was creepy. Let's get away from here."

As they rode away, Sarah said, "Zeke, there's something funny about her, about this whole thing. I want to go back there and look around. There was some kind of building behind the house. Let's sneak back."

They rode to the end of the block and left their bikes. Then they walked back toward the Bowen property, not along the street this time, but behind the row of houses. They walked in the long grass at the edge of the bean field. A barbed wire fence separated them from the back yards of the houses on the block. Sarah thought how easy it would be for someone to lead a pony back here without any of the neighbors seeing.

As they approached the last yard, Sarah's heart shook her whole body with its beating.

The back of the Bowen property was a contrast in black and green. Charred planks lay in a heap where a small barn or shed had stood. A few trees and bushes, burned black, stood out starkly against the green of this year's grass and leaves.

A small garage stood at the edge of the property, well away from the blackened part of the yard. It was almost hidden by lilac bushes. The door was shut, but there was a small

window in the back. As Sarah looked, something behind the window moved.

"There's something in there." Sarah grabbed Zeke's arm.

"In that garage?"

"Yeah. Come on."

Together they moved forward, keeping close to each other for courage. When they reached the garage wall, they crept to the window and looked in.

It was too dark inside to be sure, but something was in there. Something big. An animal. It turned toward them.

Panda saw Sarah's face at the window, and the pony whinnied.

6. The Captive

Panda blinked in the brightness of the sunlight as Sarah led her out. She still wore her bridle, and one Indian feather was left in her mane. It dangled sadly from its rubber band just behind Panda's ear.

"She's all right. She's safe. We found her." For the moment it was all Sarah could think of. All she could do was hug Panda's neck, feel her skin, smell her fragrance.

"But how in the heck—" Zeke broke off suddenly.

Sarah looked up. The woman from the trailer was frowning at them from an overgrown gravel path.

"You children put that pony back," she said sternly. "You mustn't play with Panda when Julie's not here. You come back when Julie's home, and she'll give you a ride."

Sarah stared, speechless.

"This is my pony," she managed finally. "This is Panda, the one I was asking about. You had her all the time. You must have taken her."

Sarah was suddenly aware that Zeke was slipping away. He faded into the bushes out of sight. For an instant she felt panic, but then she understood. "Go for help, Zeke," she thought. "Quick."

She turned toward the woman and said, "Are you Mrs. Bowen?" "Stall for time," she told herself. "We need help with this. Hurry, Zeke."

"Yes, that's right," the woman said. Her

voice still carried an undercurrent of pleasantness, as though she were merely scolding neighborhood children.

Sarah pulled in a big breath. "My name is Sarah Elgin. This pony does belong to me, Mrs. Bowen. My father bought her at the auction barn. See? See this feather? I was riding her in the pet parade. I was dressed up like an Indian princess. I saw you in the park, and you spoke to Panda."

The woman came closer toward Panda. Sarah tensed, but the hand only stroked Panda's neck. At close range Sarah could see something missing in the woman's expression. There was a vague softness in her eyes; yet something was missing.

Mrs. Bowen spoke. "I remember the pet parade. Julie was in it. She rode her pony, Panda. I fixed up an Indian costume for her. But it was time to go home, and she didn't come." The woman's voice broke, and her face showed the pain she felt.

Sarah reached out to pat the woman's arm. She didn't understand any of this, but she did understand pain and the need to comfort the one in pain.

Mrs. Bowen regained her voice. "Julie didn't come," she said firmly, "so I brought the pony home. Julie will be back any time now. You're a nice girl. I'm sure Julie will let you ride on Panda when she gets here."

"Mrs. Bowen," Sarah said softly, "I'm going to take Panda home now. She belongs to me."

The woman stiffened suddenly and became fierce. "No," she shouted. "You can't! If you take Panda, I'll never see Julie again. Get your hands off Panda. Get away from here."

Sarah made a jump to get on Panda's back, but it was too high and Sarah was too shaken. She didn't get on the pony. Panda jumped aside nervously, for she sensed the electricity of human emotions.

Sarah grabbed the pony's mane and tried to jump on Panda again, but Mrs. Bowen caught her. Sarah fell among Panda's legs. She rolled away, trying to dodge the dancing hooves.

Then Sarah heard voices. A man in a blue uniform appeared. Zeke and other people were behind him.

Screaming and weeping, Mrs. Bowen was held up between the policeman and a neighbor woman. "Julie, Julie," she cried.

Another neighbor appeared and led Mrs. Bowen through the hedge toward her kitchen.

The policeman was beside Sarah. He helped her to her feet and brushed her off.

"Are you okay, honey?" he asked.

Sarah nodded, dazed by the blur of events.

"This is my pony," she said, feeling that some explanation was called for.

"I know. It's all right. You're free to take your pony home now. Are you sure you're okay? We can give you a ride home in the squad car and send someone after the pony."

Sarah shook her head. Her arm was around Panda's neck, and she didn't intend to let go of that neck, ever again.

"What—what—" Sarah waved toward the house next door, where Mrs. Bowen had disappeared.

"Let's get you home first," the officer said. "We can talk later. You want to ride that pony home?"

Sarah nodded.

"All right. I'll give you a boost up."

"Son," he said to Zeke, "you go along with her, will you? See that she gets home okay. She's been shaken up, I know."

He helped Sarah up onto Panda's back. Then he asked, "You're the Elgin girl, right? I know where you live. I'll check on things here. Then I'll pick up your bike, and I'll stop out at your house later on. Okay?"

Sarah nodded, too dazed to answer. The policeman had a smile on his face as he watched Sarah and Zeke riding away, Zeke on his bike and Sarah on her beloved pony.

7. Home Again

They sat in lawn chairs in the shady side yard, so that Sarah and Panda could be close together. When Mr. Elgin had heard the news, he had driven home from his real estate office. Now he sat in a lawn chair, looking a bit out of place in his business suit. Mrs. Elgin had brought coffee from the kitchen and had settled beside her husband. Sarah sat on the grass and held Panda's lead rope while the pony ate lawn grass. It was clear that Panda had had little to eat since she was stolen.

Lieutenant Halverson balanced his coffee

cup easily on one knee. His partner sat with Zeke in the squad car and explained how the siren and police radio worked.

"So you see," Lieutenant Halverson said, "the fire was quite a tragedy. Mrs. Bowen's husband died trying to save the little girl. The child, Julie, had run into the barn to save her pony." He looked toward Panda.

There was a silence, and then Mrs. Elgin said softly, "Could you tell us about the fire?"

Lieutentant Halverson said, "It happened last November. The Bowens had been raking leaves and burning them. It was too windy to burn leaves safely, and the fire got out of control. It caught the house first. It was a very old wooden house, and it burned quickly.

"Everyone was rushing around, trying to save the house, when the wind changed direction and began blowing the fire toward the little barn where Panda was. Evidently Julie saw the barn starting to burn. She ran to get Panda out, not knowing that the pony, who had smelled the smoke, had kicked down the door at the back of the building and had bolted out that way. The pony was unhurt except for a cut of some kind, as I recall."

Sarah looked at her mother. "That scar—"

"Go on," Mrs. Elgin said to the lieutenant, bracing herself for the worst part of the story.

"Well, ma'am, the rest happened too fast to know for sure. Julie ran into the barn. Her father saw her and ran in after her, to get her out. Just then some burning trash or leaves blew against a gasoline can that was in the barn. It exploded, and the barn went up in flames instantly."

"That's enough," Mrs. Elgin interrupted. Then, as if to turn all their thoughts away from the tragedy, she said, "I still don't understand why Mrs. Bowen took Panda from the park. And I don't see how she could have walked away with that pony, without anyone noticing."

The officer said, "Apparently the woman

has not recovered mentally from the tragedy. She seemed to take it all pretty well at the time, but something in her brain must have snapped. Maybe it happened when she saw Sarah riding in the parade. She must have lost her hold on reality, and thought that Sarah was Julie.

"I expect she just untied the pony and led her home. Very likely no one noticed because it would be such a normal thing for her to do. If she had acted like a thief, then probably someone would have spotted her and reported it to us. It was just so normal that nobody noticed. Nobody remembered."

"What happens now?" Sarah asked.

The officer turned not to Sarah, but to her father. "That pretty much depends on you folks. If you want, you can file charges against Mrs. Bowen. She did steal your pony, although in her mind I'm sure she believed she was taking her daughter's pet home."

Mr. and Mrs. Elgin looked at each other

and shook their heads. Mr. Elgin said, "We don't want to file any charges. The poor woman has been through enough."

Lieutenant Halverson smiled, and stood up. "I'm glad to hear that you feel that way. Mrs. Bowen's sister is on her way over from Albia to take care of her. I'm sure Mrs. Bowen won't be bothering you folks anymore."

Softly Sarah said, "I'm sorry for her and about Julie and her father."

"Yes. Well," Lieutenant Halverson's hand rested for an instant on Sarah's head. Then the officers and the car were gone.

"Hey," Zeke said, "You promised me a ride on Panda. How about it?"

The sadness in the air seemed to break and float away. Together Sarah and Zeke led Panda toward the stable. Their laughter filled the sunny morning, and Mr. and Mrs. Elgin exchanged a long, loving look.